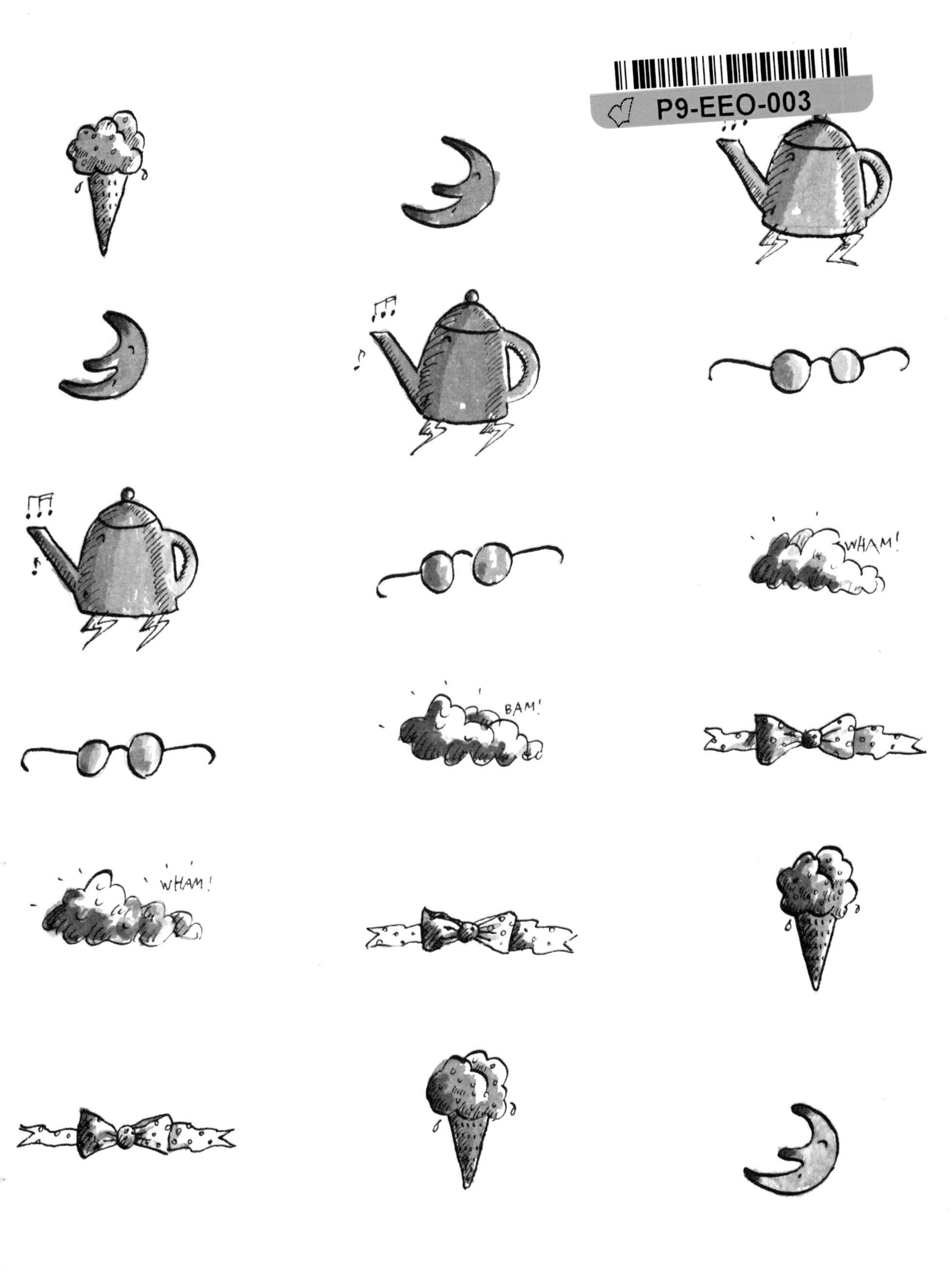
WHAM!
BAM!
WHAM!

WHAM!
BAM!

MAGNOLIA'S MIXED-UP Magic

by Joan Lowery Nixon

pictures by Linda Bucholtz-Ross

G. P. Putnam's Sons New York

 Published simultaneously in
Canada by General Publishing Co. Limited, Toronto.
Printed in the United States of America.
Library of Congress Cataloging in Publication Data
Nixon, Joan Lowery.
Magnolia's mixed-up magic.
Summary: An old book of magic enables Magnolia
Possum and her grandmother to experiment with
spells while unaware that the pages containing
instructions on how to undo them are missing.
[1. Opossums—Fiction. 2. Animals—Fiction. 3. Magic—Fiction]
I. Bucholtz-Ross, Linda, ill. II. Title.
PZ7.N65Mag 1983 [Fic] 82-16684
ISBN 0-399-20956-5
Second impression

FOR OUR OWN
'MAGNOLIA BLOSSOM'
MAUREEN,
WITH LOVE

KACHOO!
RECIPES
CHEF'S CHOICE
POSSUM GOURMET

ONE

Magnolia Possum opened her grandma's kitchen door and sniffed. She had hoped to smell cinnamon cookies and apple pudding. But instead she sniffed a strange, dry odor. She sneezed.

"Bless you!" Grandma Possum said. She gave Magnolia a hug. "Come see what I found for you. It was in with those dusty old books on the top shelf of Mrs. Fox's store."

She picked up a book. Dust flew from the pages. This time Grandma sneezed, and her glasses bounced to the end of her nose.

"Bless me, too," she said. "Magnolia, this is a very old and special book."

The book didn't look special to Magnolia, but it did look old. Its cover was ragged and dirty.

"What kind of a book is it?" Magnolia asked. She looked closely at the cover. On it she read: *A True Book of Magic Spells.*

"I haven't read it yet," Grandma said. "But it's all about how to do magic. And I know you love those magic shows on the TV."

Magnolia dragged a high-backed wooden chair up to the kitchen table. She climbed onto it and rested her chin on the checkered tablecloth. "Let's do some magic," she said.

Grandma pulled her chair up to the table. She pushed her glasses up and opened the book. "Not so fast, Magnolia honey," she said. "We can't just go jumping into magic. We have to read up on it first."

She ran her finger down the first page. "Doorbells that ring and teakettles that sing."

"That isn't magic," Magnolia complained.

Grandma's eyebrows wiggled. "It is when they do it all by themselves."

HERBS
EAT RIGHT
MORE HERBS
A TRUE BOOK OF MAGIC SPELLS

"Does it have any disappearing tricks in it?" Magnolia asked. "Disappearing tricks are the best."

Grandma turned the pages carefully. The paper was yellowed and stiff and the edges were torn. Magnolia scratched her nose and thought about how much fun it would be to disappear.

Finally, Grandma said, "Here it is! *How to Make Someone Disappear.*"

Magnolia bounced up and down in her chair. "Try it, Grandma! Make me disappear!"

Before Grandma could answer there was a loud knock on the kitchen door.

The door opened and Mr. Bernard Beaver poked his head into the kitchen. He took off his postman's cap and wiped his forehead. "A good, good morning to y'all," he said. "Got something for you. Two bills, a magazine,

and a letter from your cousin, Mary Nell, in Sweetwater."

"Come on in, Bernard," Grandma said. "I want to show you something."

Mr. Beaver put his mailbag on the end of the table. "I sure would like a glass of iced tea if you've got one handy," he said. "My throat couldn't feel any more dry and scratchy if I were eating stale potato chips in a sandstorm."

Grandma poured three glasses of iced tea and they each

took one. "Look at that book on the table," she said. "It's full of magic tricks."

"I never in my life saw any magic tricks," Bernard told them. "Mama always says that sawing people in half and making them disappear is just a lot of foolishness for folks who don't have something better to do."

Grandma put down her glass of tea. "While you're drinking your tea, I'm going to wrap up a little something for Mary Nell so you can take it to the post office."

She left the kitchen and Magnolia said, "This book tells how to do real magic."

Mr. Beaver took a long swallow of tea. "Don't tell me about magic. Tell Mrs. Fox. She could use some magic to keep her store from getting robbed. Poor lady. It happened to her twice last month."

Magnolia pulled the book toward her. "Would you like to see me make someone disappear?" she asked Mr. Beaver.

Mr. Beaver laughed. "Sure. I'll watch your little magic game, long as I have to wait for your grandma anyway."

Magnolia read the magic spell in a slow, solemn voice:

"Dirty socks and ginger-beer,
Icky, sticky, disappear!"

As she read the last word, she pointed at Bernard Beaver and said, "Abracadabra!"

Wham! There was a sound like thunder and the room was filled with such a bright light Magnolia squeezed her eyes shut.

When she opened them, Mr. Beaver was gone.

TWO

Grandma hurried into the kitchen, carrying her package. "What was that terrible noise?" she asked. "And where did Mr. Beaver go?"

"What do you mean, where am I?" said a voice. "I'm right here."

"But I can't see you," Grandma said.

"I think I made him disappear!" Magnolia shouted. She was so excited she could hardly speak.

Mr. Beaver gasped. "You mean no one can see me? Mama will never believe that!"

"Mercy me!" Grandma said. "I'm right sorry about this, Bernard. I'll look in that book this very minute and find out how to undo the magic spell."

"No hurry. Let's think on this a minute," Mr. Beaver said. "Mama always says that behind every lemon meringue pie is a sour lemon."

"What does that mean?" Magnolia asked.

"It means that what seems sour might turn out to be good. I'd kind of like to stay this way for a while. There's a little yappy dog that hangs around the neighborhood. He follows me and yaps at me till I think my ears will pop. I'd like to walk right past him and know he can't see me."

He took the package from Grandma and put it in his mailbag. He picked up the mailbag and slung it on his shoulder. All Magnolia could see was a mailbag sailing out the door.

"Oh, mercy!" Grandma said again. She plopped into her chair by the table. "I don't think we were ready for that much magic. I told you, Magnolia, that we should start at the beginning."

She pulled the book toward her and pushed her glasses up again. "See—right here," she said. "Clocks that are ticking and lights that are flicking."

"That's not magic," Magnolia said.

"It is if there weren't any clocks or lights there to begin with," Grandma said. She turned a page. " 'How to make someone float in the air.' No. I think we should go back to the ringing doorbells."

Magnolia hopped out of her chair. "Grandma! You mean you could make me float in the air?"

"After we try some of the simple tricks."

"But singing teakettles and ticking clocks aren't any fun. Just think how lovely it would be to float in the air."

"Well," Grandma said. "I suppose we could give it a try."

She found the right page and read:

"Squishy shoes and leaky boat,
Glucky, wucky, now you float!
Abracadabra!"

The thunder made a terrible racket and the bright lights flashed. When it was over, Magnolia found herself gently rising up to the ceiling.

"Grandma!" she cried. "This is wonderful."

"My stars! We did it!" Grandma said.

Magnolia pushed herself through the air. It was like swimming. She brushed a cobweb from a corner and sailed back and forth across the room.

"Try floating, Grandma," Magnolia said. "You'll like it!"

"It does look like fun," Grandma said.

"Bring me down, and this time I'll be the magician and make you float," Magnolia said.

Grandma picked up the book again. She began turning pages. When she got to the end she dropped back into her chair and groaned.

"Magnolia honey," she said, "this is terrible. The back pages of the book are missing. There's nothing to tell how to undo the magic spells."

AHH!
OH!
OOH!

"You mean I have to stay up here?" Magnolia asked. "And no one will ever be able to see Mr. Beaver again?"

All Grandma could answer was, "Oh, mercy mercy me."

THREE

Magnolia rolled over on her back, high above the kitchen table. "Please don't feel bad, Grandma," she said. "It was my fault."

"What are we going to do?" Grandma asked.

"I like it up here, Grandma. I really do," Magnolia said. "And I think Mr. Beaver is glad that no one can see him, especially that yappy dog."

"But your mother and father aren't going to like it," Grandma said. "And I don't think Bernard's mama is going to be very happy about it."

Magnolia looked out the window. She wondered what it would be like to float out in the breeze. "Let's go down to Mrs. Fox's store and look for the missing pages," she said.

"We can't go outside," Grandma said. "You might float away."

"I'll tie a long ribbon around my waist," Magnolia said, "and you can hold the other end. I'll be just like a balloon."

"I suppose it's better than sitting here fretting," Grandma said.

She found a long ribbon in her sewing drawer. She tied it around Magnolia's waist and they walked out the door.

A little gust of wind pushed Magnolia this way and that. It was like being rocked in a boat. She giggled and ducked under a tree branch as they reached the sidewalk.

"My goodness! What is that up ahead of us?" Grandma cried.

Magnolia did a somersault so she could see what her Grandma was staring at. In the air, just above the sidewalk, a mailbag was bouncing up and down.

"It's Mr. Beaver," she said. "And look. There's a little dog following him."

"Wait up, Bernard!" Grandma called, and the mailbag stopped.

''I suppose Magnolia's up there doing another magic trick,'' Mr. Beaver said. ''But if she's fixing to go around town like that, people will start to talk.''

''It's just for a while,'' Magnolia said.

''Say! I just thought of something. How'd y'all know it was me? I thought y'all couldn't see me,'' Mr. Beaver said.

''We can't see you. But we can see your mailbag,'' Grandma told him.

He laughed. ''That's all this little yappy dog can see, and he's mighty puzzled.''

''There's something I'd better tell you, Bernard,'' Grandma said. ''But first come along with us to Mrs. Fox's store.''

''That's just where I'm heading,'' he said. ''I'm going to take Mrs. Fox a catalogue and a postcard from her Uncle Bubba, who's visiting in California and having a fine time for himself.''

Grandma was the first to reach the screen door to Mrs. Fox's store. She pushed it open and Magnolia floated through.

Magnolia didn't stop to enjoy the cool air from the slow ceiling fans or the smells of ripe apples and peppermint candy and spicy pickles. She didn't have time.

Mrs. Fox was standing behind the counter, a frightened look on her face. On the other side of the counter was a sharp-faced raccoon, his bright eyes peering through a black mask.

"Oh, no!" Magnolia shouted. "Mrs. Fox is being robbed again!"

FOUR

Magnolia gave a tug on the ribbon to free herself from Grandma's grasp. She dived toward the robber.

She was scared, but the robber looked scared, too, as he watched Magnolia fly toward him.

"Get out of here!" she screeched at the robber.

"A flying possum?" he shouted.

MRS. FOX
HAVE
SUNNY FARM
POSSUM GROVE CO-OP
US MAIL

“I’ll get that robber.” Mr. Beaver’s voice boomed through the store, and his mailbag began swinging in the air as it rushed toward the robber.

The robber yelled and dashed toward the door, stomping on the little yappy dog’s tail.

The dog yelped and chased the robber out the door and into the street.

Grandma grabbed Magnolia's ribbon and pulled her down near the counter.

The swinging door opened and the yappy dog came back in. He sat by the door with his tail wagging. His mouth was clamped on a piece of the robber's pants.

The receiver lifted off the wall phone and hung in the air. Then Mr. Beaver's voice said, "Police! Look for a

HELLO, POLICE?
THE COUNTRY LIFE
HERBS
WATER BISCUITS
23
US MAIL
THE FOX FINDER

robber with a black mask and a big hole in his pants.''

''This has been a very strange day,'' Mrs. Fox said to Grandma. ''It must be the heat.'' She looked with wide eyes at Magnolia, who floated over the cash register. She stared at the hanging mailbag and watched the receiver go back to its place on the wall phone.

''We've been trying a little magic,'' Grandma said to Mrs. Fox.

''I can see that,'' Mrs. Fox said. ''You've got a balloon that looks and sounds like Magnolia. And a mailbag that floats in the air and talks on the phone. And a dog that chases robbers.''

''Not exactly,'' Grandma said. ''That balloon really is Magnolia. Say hello, Magnolia.''

''Hi,'' Magnolia said.

Grandma sighed. ''I wish someone had a good idea of how to undo these magic tricks.''

''You mean I've got to stay like this?'' Mr. Beaver asked. He sounded upset.

''Don't fret, Bernard,'' Grandma said. ''Just help us try to think of what to do next.''

''Where did you find the magic book?'' Magnolia asked her grandma. ''Maybe the missing pages are still on the shelf.''

"On the top shelf," Grandma said. "A little to the right," she added as she watched Magnolia look through the dusty books piled on the shelf.

Magnolia finally shook her head and floated over the counter. "Mrs. Fox," she said, "the book Grandma bought from you has some pages missing."

"I don't want my customers to be unhappy. I'll give your grandma her money back," Mrs. Fox said.

"But we need the missing pages," Magnolia said. "They tell how to undo the magic tricks."

"Hmmm." Mrs. Fox thought for a moment. "It seems to me I did find some loose pages the last time I dusted up there."

Mr. Beaver sneezed. "Which must have been a long time ago," he said.

Mrs. Fox ignored him. "I didn't know where they belonged. I didn't throw them out. I did something with them, but what it was I can't rightly say."

"Did you maybe use them to write notes on?" Bernard asked.

"Not with printing on both sides," Magnolia said.

"Did you line a drawer with them?" Grandma asked.

Mrs. Fox shook her head.

Magnolia looked around the room. From up in the air

it was easy to see everything: cans and boxes of food, brooms and mops, bottles of milk and soda pop, and the little yappy dog, who was scratching and sniffing at what looked like a hole in the wall near the floorboards. Something was in the hole.

SOAP FLAKES

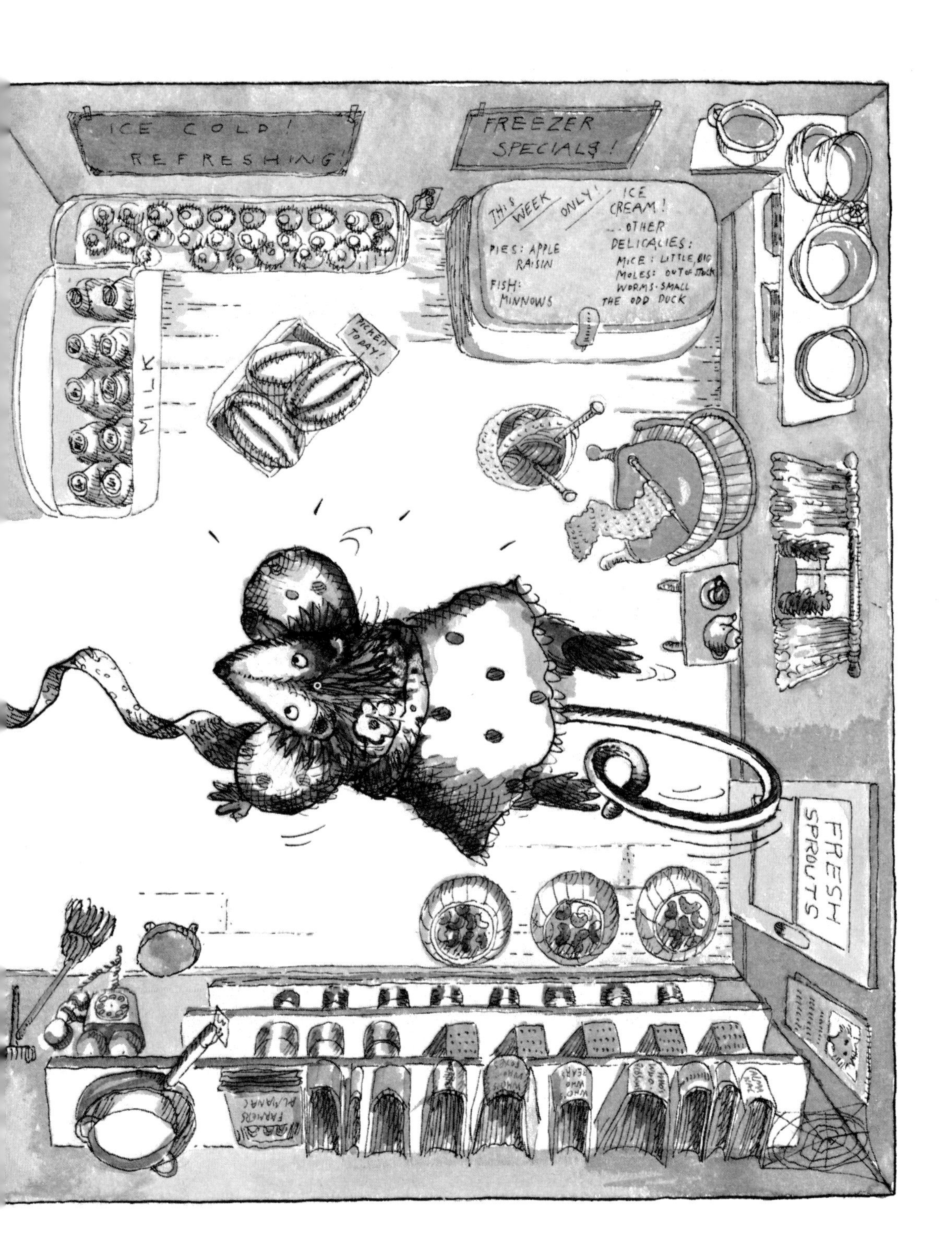
ICE COLD! REFRESHING!
FREEZER SPECIALS!
THIS WEEK ONLY! ICE CREAM! ...OTHER DELICACIES:
PIES: APPLE RAISIN
FISH: MINNOWS
MICE: LITTLE, BIG
MOLES: OUT of STOCK
WORMS. SMALL
THE ODD DUCK
PICKED TODAY!
MILK
FRESH SPROUTS
FARMERS ALMANAC

"Mrs. Fox," Magnolia said, " did you ever have mice in your store?"

"Why, yes I did," Mrs. Fox said.

"And did you find their mousehole and stuff it with something to keep them out of your store?"

Mrs. Fox's mouth opened. "Could be I did at that," she said. "I remember now. I used some pages that had fallen out of an old book."

"I think the little yappy dog smells the mousehole," Magnolia said. "He doesn't know it, but I do believe he found the missing pages from the magic book."

Grandma pulled Magnolia down and she poked her fingers into the hole. She tugged until she pulled out the wad of paper.

Magnolia looked through the pages as she slowly rose to the ceiling. "They're too badly worn and torn," she said. "All I can read is,

"To end a spell, trick or flim-flam,
Just point and shout, 'Al—' "

"Shout 'Al'?" Mr. Beaver asked. "That doesn't sound right. I know an Al over in Caney Creek, but he'd never fool around with magic."

"The page is torn," Magnolia said. "The rest of the word is gone."

Mr. Beaver sighed. "If I have to stay like this forever, my mama is going to have something to say about it."

Grandma pulled at Magnolia's ribbon. "Magnolia honey, think back to those magic shows on TV. Did anybody say anything that started with 'Al'?"

Magnolia thought a moment. Then she laughed. "Of course!" she shouted. "Alakazam!"

Bang, went the thunder! Zap, went the light! Magnolia landed with a plop on the counter. She climbed off and hugged her grandma.

"Bernard's back," Grandma said.

"I've been here all along," he said.

"Everything's taken care of except the little yappy dog who doesn't belong to anyone," Magnolia said.

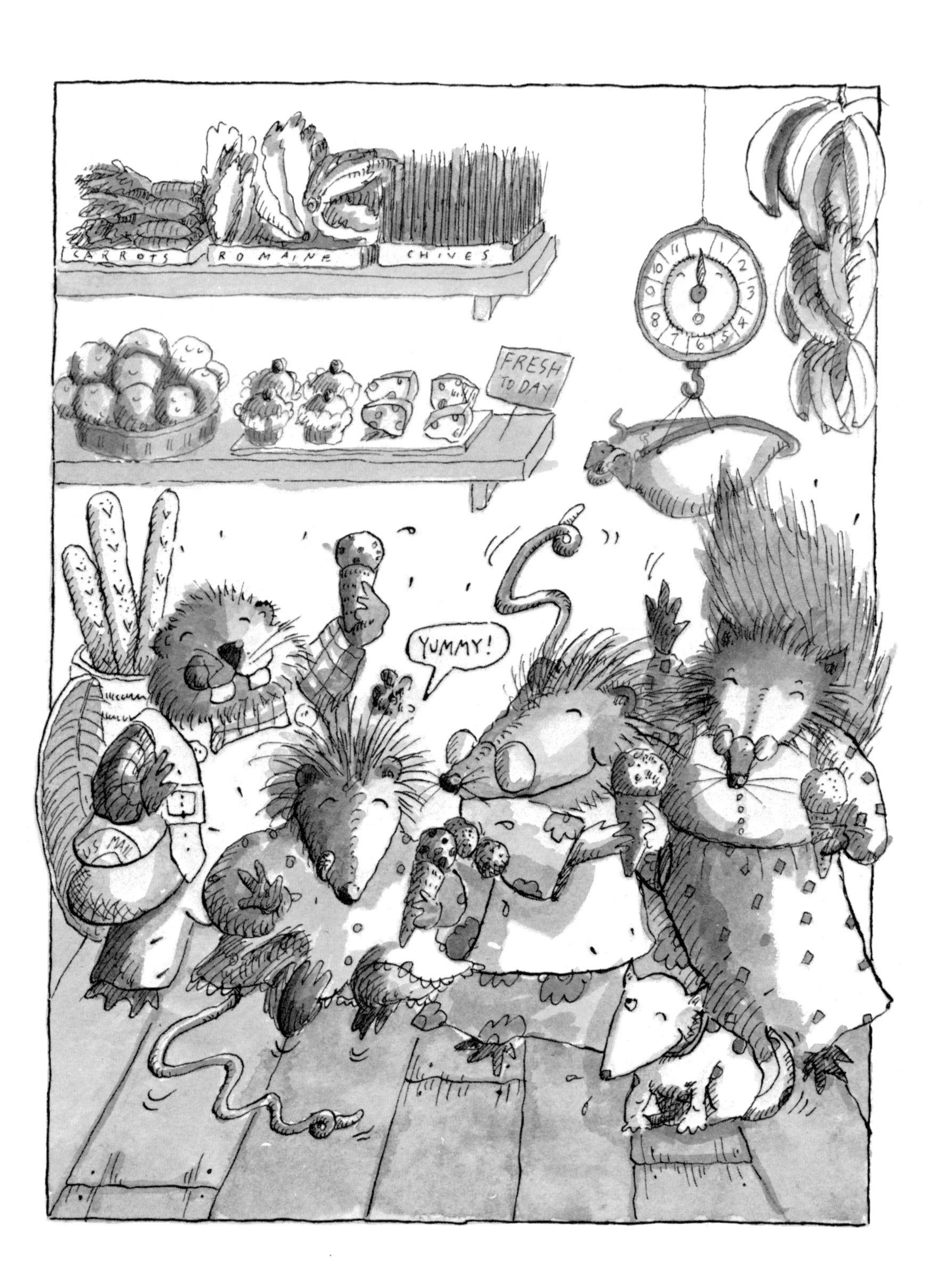
CARROTS
ROMAINE
CHIVES
FRESH TO DAY
YUMMY!
US MAIL

''I could use a yappy dog to keep chasing away robbers,'' Mrs. Fox said.

''Before we do another thing, let's celebrate with some ice cream cones,'' Grandma said.

Bernard took a step back. ''Are y'all going to try to make anything else disappear?'' he asked.

''Just the ice cream,'' Magnolia said. ''And we don't need a book of magic for that!''

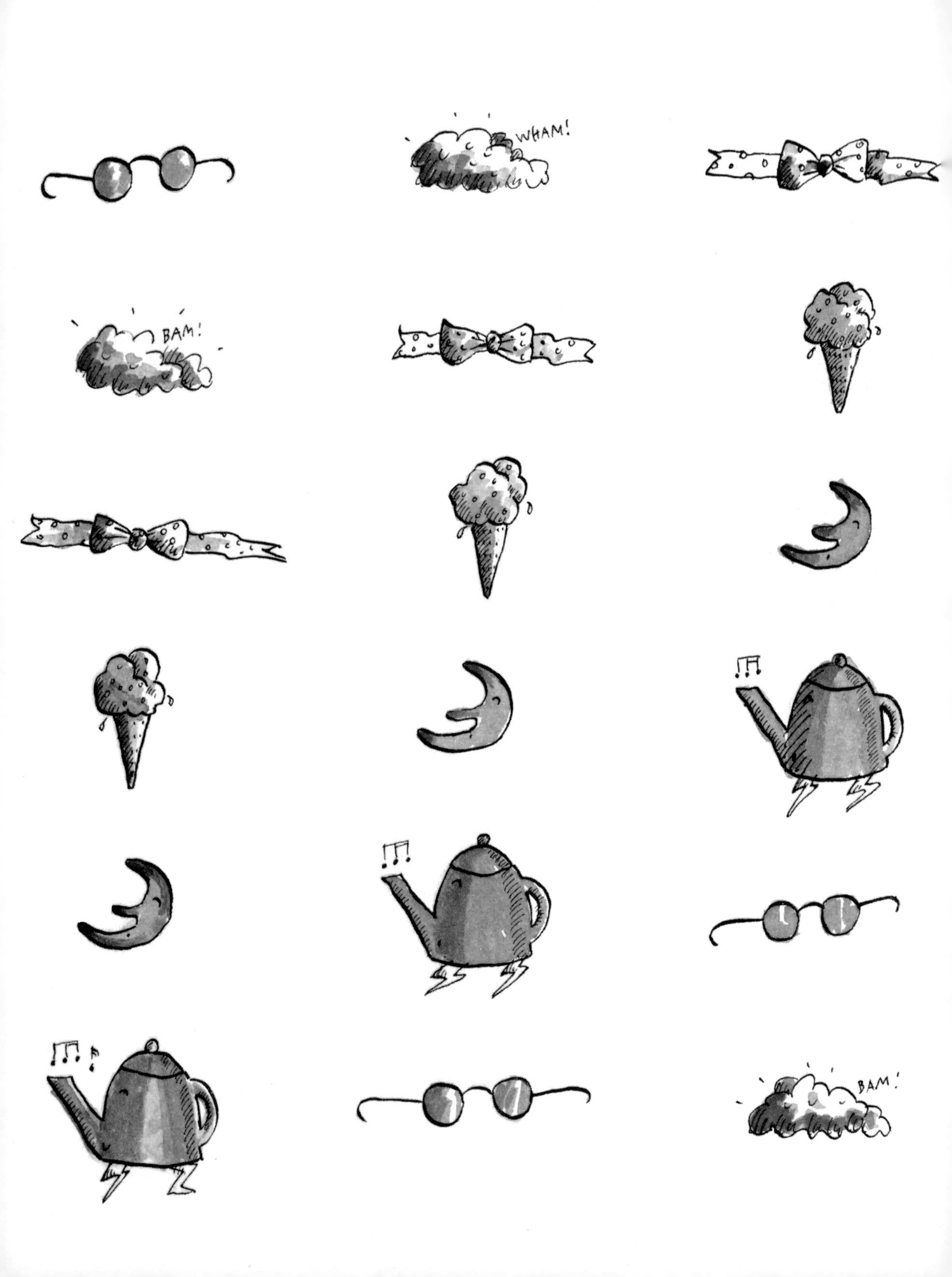
WHAM!
BAM!
BAM!